This Peppa Pig book belongs to

PRIYA

•••••••••••••••••••••••

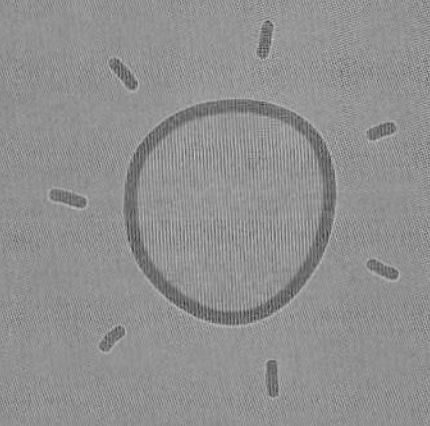

LADYBIRD BOOKS

UK | USA | Canada | Ireland | Australia
India | New Zealand | South Africa

Ladybird Books is part of the Penguin Random House group of companies
whose addresses can be found at global.penguinrandomhouse.com.

ladybird.com

First published 2015
002

Adapted by Sue Nicholson

Printed in China

A CIP catalogue record for this book is available from the British Library

ISBN: 978-0-723-29930-1

Contents

Peppa's Family

Hello! I'm Peppa Pig, and this is my little brother, George. Here are some pictures of my family and my friends. Make the sounds each time you spot one of us in the picture.

and Friends

Peppa has lots of friends – and YOU are Peppa's friend, too!

Story Time

Horsey Twinkle Toes

Peppa and George are playing in their bedroom.
"Dine-saw! Grrrrr!" says George.
Just then, the doorbell rings. Ding-dong!

It's Mr Zebra the Postman with a parcel.
"It's probably that box of reinforced concrete I ordered," says Daddy Pig.
But it's not Daddy Pig's reinforced concrete.
It's a parcel for Peppa and George!
"Look at all those stamps!" says Peppa.

"A parcel! How exciting!" says Mummy Pig.
The parcel has come from Aunty Dottie, who lives in a different country, far away. She has sent a letter, too. It says:

Dear Peppa and George,
Here is a present for you to share.
Love from your Aunty Dottie

Peppa and her family open the parcel.
The present has wheels, legs, a tail and a handle.
"Whatever can it be?" asks Mummy Pig.
There's one last thing in the box . . .

It's a toy horse!
"I shall call it Twinkle Toes!" says Peppa.
"Horsey!" says George.
"Twinkle Toes!" says Peppa.
"Horsey!" says George.
"Twinkle Toes!"
"Horsey!"
"Twinkle Toes!"
"Horsey!"

"The present is for BOTH of you!" says Daddy Pig.
"You will have to share it. Sharing can be fun!"

Peppa and George take turns.
George is the youngest, so he gets to go first.
"Horsey!"
George likes playing with Horsey.

Next it's Peppa's turn.
"I'm Princess Peppa with my magic horse, Twinkle Toes!"
Peppa likes playing with Twinkle Toes.
CRASH! Peppa knocks over some boxes in the hallway.
"I think you should play outside where there's more space," says Mummy Pig.

Daddy Pig thinks it's a bit steep for Peppa and George to play near the house.
"I'll just ride it down to the bottom of the hill!" he says.
"Be careful, Daddy," shouts Peppa.
Whoa!

Daddy Pig goes too fast and lands in the duck pond!
"Silly Daddy," says Peppa.
"Did you know you have a duck on your head?" asks Mummy Pig.
Snort! Snort! Hee! Hee!

George tries to ride Horsey, but he can't make it go.
"Oh dear! If only there was someone big and strong to push him . . ."
begins Daddy Pig.
"ME!" shouts Peppa. "I'm big and strong. I can push George!"

Peppa pushes George round and round the duck pond.
"Horsey!" says George.
"Twinkle Toes!" says Peppa.
It is lots of fun.
"I know," says Peppa. "Because the present's for both of us, let's call it . . .
Horsey Twinkle Toes!"
"What a good idea!" say Mummy and Daddy Pig.

Piggy Playtime

Peppa and George have lots of fun playing together on Horsey Twinkle Toes. Can you help them spot all the things in the garden?

Colour in the box next to each thing as you find it.

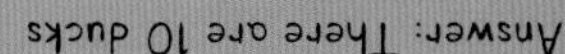

How many ducks can you see?

Write the number here. ☐

Pony Puzzle

Can you put these four pictures in order to tell the story of how Peppa and her family built Horsey Twinkle Toes? Write the numbers 1, 2, 3 and 4 in the circles next to each picture.

Do you like the name Horsey Twinkle Toes?
What would you call your toy horse?

Answer: 2, 3, 4, 1

Odd Toy Out

Here are some of Peppa and George's favourite toys. Can you spot the odd one out in each row?

Answers: 1. d, 2. b, 3. e, 4. b, 5. c

Pick the Parcel!

Mr Zebra the Postman has delivered lots of parcels to Peppa and her friends. Answer the questions by pointing to the right place in the picture.

Which is the biggest parcel?

Which is the smallest parcel?

Can you find a big blue stamp?

Who is carrying the most parcels?

Which parcel has three red stamps on it?

Can you read the name written on the smallest parcel?

Who is not holding a parcel?

George's Dinosaurs

George loves dinosaurs! Help him match the dinosaurs to their shadow shapes.

1

2

3

4

a

b

c

d

Answers: 1. b, 2. a, 3. d, 4. c

Paint with Peppa

Peppa loves painting! Can you colour in the picture using the colour key?

What is Peppa painting?

Shake, Rattle and Bang!
Madame Gazelle is teaching Peppa and her friends about musical instruments. Can you match each instrument to the sound it makes?
1.25
1
0.75
0.5
0.25
Emily Elephant is clicking some castanets.
Peppa is banging a big bass drum.
Pedro Pony is blowing a trumpet.
Rebecca Rabbit is crashing the cymbals.
Freddy Fox is playing the triangle.
BOOM! BOOM!
Clickety-click Clickety-click
CRASH! CRASH!
Ting-a-ling-a-ling
TOOT! TOOT!
Can you make all the sounds, too?
22

Grampy's Gym Class

It's time for Grampy Rabbit's gym class. Join in the fun by copying all the actions with Peppa and her friends.

Story Time

The Blackberry Bush

Peppa and her family are at Granny and Grandpa Pig's house.
"Today, I'm going to make an apple and blackberry crumble," says Granny Pig.
"I want everyone to get the fruit for me!"
"Aye aye, Granny Pig," say Grandpa Pig, Mummy and Daddy Pig, Peppa and George.

"Getting the apples is the easy bit," says Grandpa Pig. "On the count of three, shake the tree! One . . . two . . . three . . ."
Everyone shakes the apple tree, and lots of juicy red apples PLOP to the ground.

Snort! Snort! Hee! Hee! Peppa and George have fun catching the falling apples in their baskets.

"Now for the hard bit . . ." says Grandpa Pig. "Picking the blackberries!"

The blackberry bush is very big and very thorny.
Grandpa Pig doesn't like it. "It's an overgrown weed," he says.
"Silly Grandpa!" says Mummy Pig. "It has lots of juicy blackberries! This bush has been here since I was a little piggy," she tells Peppa and George.

Grandpa Pig uses his long stick to hook down a branch so George can pick some blackberries without getting tangled.
"Clever Grandpa!" says Peppa.

Mummy Pig has brought a ladder so she can climb right to the top of the bush!
"The juiciest blackberries are up here!" she says.
"Be careful, Mummy Pig!" everyone shouts.

Whoa! Mummy Pig falls right into the middle of the blackberry bush!

Soon Suzy Sheep arrives.
"My mummy is having an adventure," says Peppa. "She is stuck in a thorny bush, just like Sleeping Beauty!"
"Oooh," says Suzy. "I wish my mummy would have an adventure!"

Peppa tells everyone the story of Sleeping Beauty . . .

"Once upon a time, a princess called Sleeping Beauty fell asleep in a thorny bush. She stayed there for one hundred years until she was rescued by a handsome prince who gave her a kiss."

“I will rescue Mummy Pig!” says Daddy Pig.
Daddy Pig cuts away the thorny brambles with Grandpa Pig’s pruning shears and rescues Mummy Pig.
“My handsome prince,” says Mummy Pig – and she gives Daddy Pig a big kiss.

“Look! My mummy is a blackberry bush!” says Peppa.
“Let’s pick her!” says Grandpa Pig.
Everyone picks Mummy Pig’s juicy blackberries.
“I thought this sort of thing only happened to me!” laughs Daddy Pig.

"I never want to see another blackberry in my life!" Mummy Pig tells Granny Pig when they get back to the house.
"Even in an apple and blackberry crumble?" asks Granny Pig.
Mummy Pig tries a spoonful of crumble. "Delicious!" she says.

Mummy Pig loves Granny Pig's apple and blackberry crumble!

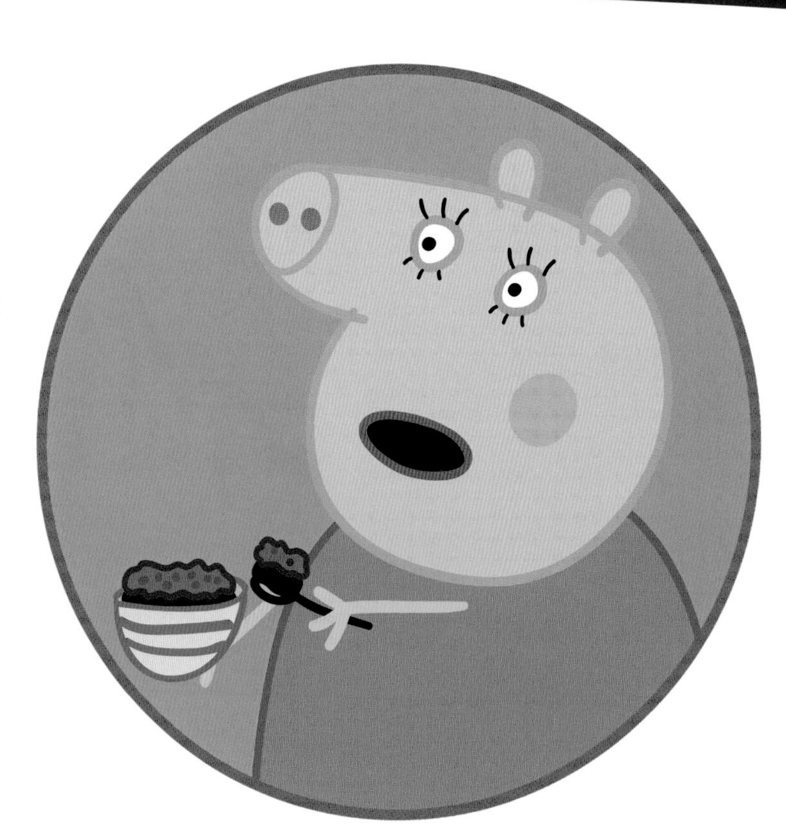

Everyone loves Granny Pig's apple and blackberry crumble!
Yum! Yum!

Hooks and Ladders

Peppa and George love playing board games. This game is for two or more players. It's just like Snakes and Ladders, but you slide down long hooks instead of slippery snakes!

24 25 26

23 22 21

12 13 14

11 10 9

START 1 2

You will need

- a dice
- counters (one for each person)

How to play

1. Starting with the youngest player, take it in turns to roll the dice and move round the board.
2. If you land on the top of a hook, slide down to the bottom.
3. If you land on the bottom of a ladder, climb to the top.
4. The player who reaches the finish first is the winner!

Counting Fun

Help Peppa and George count all the apples and blackberries growing in Grandpa Pig's garden. Write the answers in the boxes.

Who has picked the most apples – Peppa or George?

Answers: There are 23 apples and 10 blackberries. George has picked the most apples

Daddy Pig to the Rescue!

Help Daddy Pig find his way to the middle of the thorny blackberry bush to rescue Mummy Pig.

START

My brave prince!

Spot the Difference

Here are two pictures of everyone enjoying Granny Pig's delicious apple and blackberry crumble. Can you spot six differences between the pictures?

Colour in a bowl each time you spot a difference.

Answers: 1. Clock, 2. Grandpa Pig's bowl, 3. Kitchen tap, 4. Mummy Pig's mouth, 5. Picture on the calendar, 6. Fridge magnet

Sleeping Piggy

Here's Princess Peppa fast asleep like Sleeping Beauty.
What do you think Peppa is dreaming about?
Draw a picture of Peppa's dream.

Can you tell the story of Sleeping Beauty? Start with the words "Once upon a time . . ."

Grandpa Pig is planting some vegetables in his garden. Draw a circle round all the things he will need.

Answers: Some seeds, a rake, a wheelbarrow, a watering can and a spade

Beautiful Butterflies

Look at these beautiful fluttering butterflies!
Finish colouring in each butterfly's wings so they match.

One insect on this page is not a butterfly. Can you point to it?
Trace over the dotted lines to spell what it is called.

It's a fuzzy, buzzy bee.

Paper Aeroplanes

Mummy Pig is showing Peppa and George how to make paper aeroplanes. Ask a grown-up to help you follow the instructions to make your own paper aeroplanes – all you need is some old paper.

What to do

1 Fold the paper down the middle.

2 Fold the corners in at the top, so they meet in the middle.

3 Fold those corners in again, to make a point.

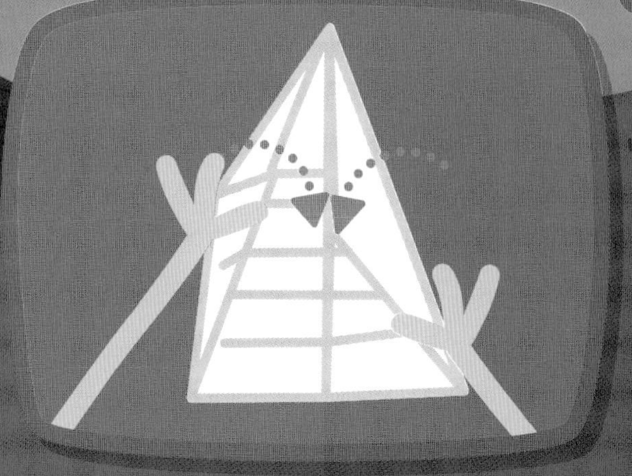

Trace over the dotted lines with your finger to see where each aeroplane has landed.

Look! George's aeroplane has done a loop-the-loop!

4 Fold the shape in half down the middle.

5 Fold each side down from the centre to the sides, so the long edges line up.

6 Hold your plane like this.

Answers: Mummy Pig's aeroplane has landed in a tree, Peppa's has landed in a flower pot, and George's has landed in the duck pond!

Rainy Day Rhyme

Here's a poem about Peppa and George. When you see a picture, say the word next to it in the key.

Key Peppa George rain snow sun

and want to play

But look outside, it's today!

"No!" says Peppa. "No! No! No!"

Now the has turned to

Never mind, here comes the

and have lots of fun!

Finish colouring in the picture of Peppa and George jumping up and down in muddy puddles.

Brr! It's a cold, snowy day! Help Daddy Pig find his woolly hat and scarf.

What have Peppa and George made in the snow?

Summertime I-Spy

It's a lovely hot, sunny day and Peppa and her family are at the beach. Lots of Peppa's friends are there, too. Can you spy all the things in the picture beginning with the letter "s"?

Practise writing the letter "s" by tracing over the dotted lines.

Sandcastle

Suzy Sheep

Starfish
Sun
Seashell
Spade

Treasure Trove

Look! Peppa and her friends have found some treasure buried in the sand. Use the key to colour in the jewels.

Pizza, Pizza, Pie!

Look at all this delicious food! Can you help Peppa draw what comes next in each row?

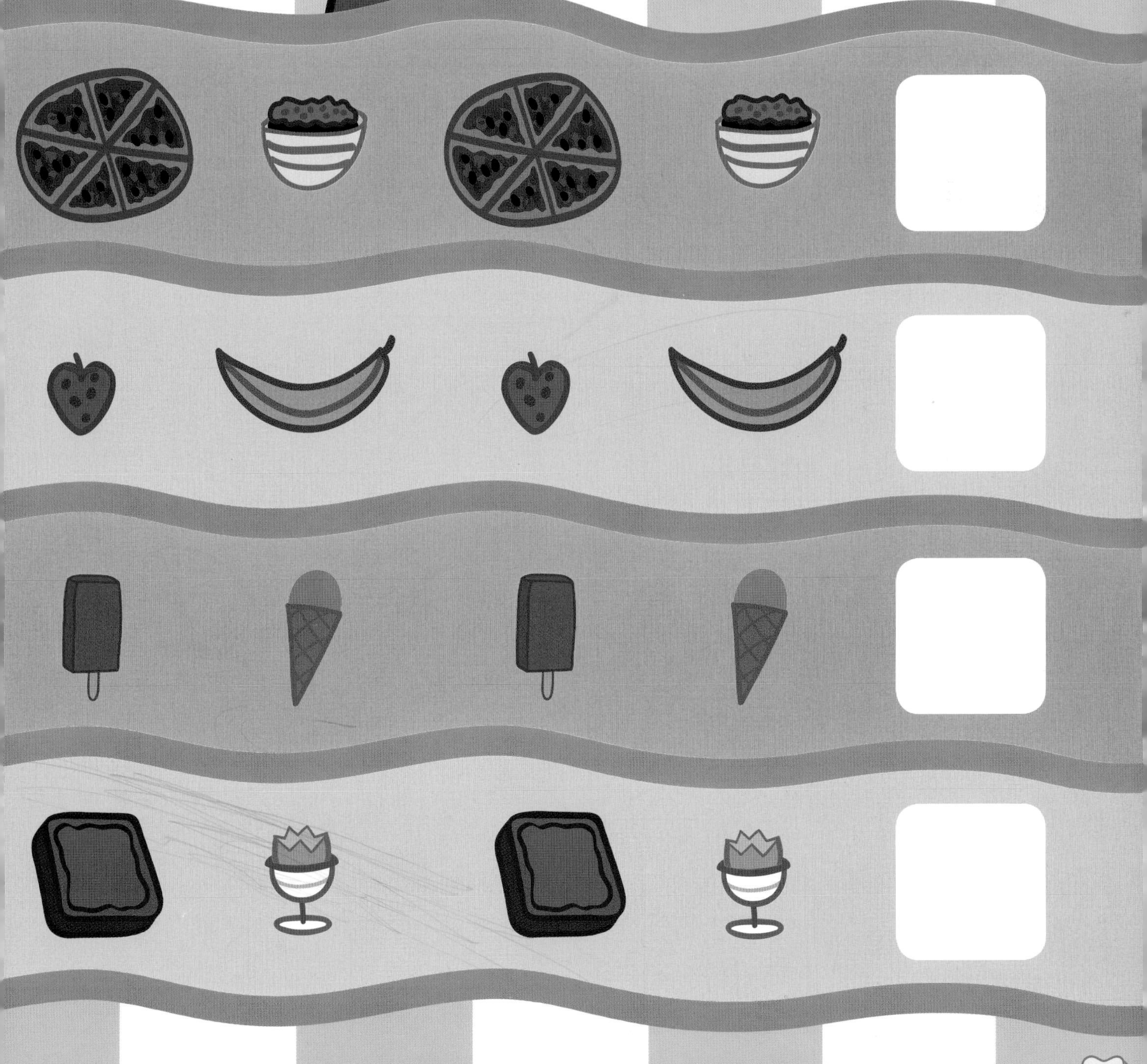

Answers: Pizza, strawberry, ice lolly, toast

Pirate Party

Yo-ho-ho! Today is Danny Dog's pirate party! Peppa and her friends love dressing up – but not all of these fancy dress costumes are pirate costumes. Draw a circle round the pirate costume in each row.

Do you like fancy dress parties?
Point to your favourite dressing-up costume.

Birthday Cake Candles

Decorate and colour in Danny's birthday cake. Yum! Yum! Danny is four today. Draw four candles on Danny's cake.

Tick-tock! Match the Clock!

Match what Peppa is doing during her busy day to the different times on the clocks.

At 8 o'clock Peppa has breakfast.

At 10 o'clock Peppa goes to playgroup.

At 11 o'clock Peppa and her friends visit the space museum with Madame Gazelle.

At 1 o'clock Peppa has lunch with Granny and Grandpa Pig.

At 3 o'clock Peppa plays in the garden with George.

At 7 o'clock Peppa gets ready for bed.

At 8 o'clock Shh! Peppa is fast asleep.

Draw the hands on these clocks to match the times.

2 o'clock

4 o'clock

8 o'clock

10 o'clock

Story Time

Digging Up the Road

It is a lovely sunny day. Peppa and her family are driving to the playground.
"Is everyone ready?" shouts Daddy Pig.
"Yes!"
"Then off we go!"
Peppa and George love going to the playground.

Oh dear! Daddy Pig has stopped the car.
"Why have we stopped?" asks Peppa.
"We're in a traffic jam!" explains Daddy Pig.
George starts to cry. He wants to go to the playground.
"Don't worry, George! The traffic is moving now!" says Daddy Pig.

"STOP!"
It's Mr Bull. Mr Bull has stopped the traffic again.
"What's the problem, Mr Bull?" asks Mummy Pig.
"MOOO! WE'RE DIGGING UP THE ROAD!" says Mr Bull.

"Look!" says Peppa. "There's water coming out of the ground!"
"Yes, it's coming from a broken pipe under the road – and we're going to fix it," says Mr Bull.
"Will it take long?" asks Mummy Pig.
"It will take as long as it takes!" says Mr Bull.

First, Mr Rhino digs a hole in the road with his digger.
"Digger! Digger!" says George.
George likes diggers.

Next, Mr Bull turns the water off, and a crane lifts out the old pipe.
"Crane! Crane!" says George.
George likes cranes.

Then the crane puts in the new pipe.
It is very exciting.
"Thank you for showing us your work, Mr Bull!" says Mummy Pig.
"MOOOO! No problem!"

Mr Bull changes the traffic light to green – and off they go.
Oh dear! George starts to cry again.
He doesn't want to leave Mr Bull.
"But we're going to the playground, George!" says Peppa.
"You can play diggers and cranes in the sandpit," says Mummy Pig.
"And we'll see Mr Bull again on our way home," says Daddy Pig.

George stops crying.
He likes going to the playground, especially when he can play diggers and cranes in the sandpit.

Peppa and George have lots of fun at the playground.
Peppa tells her friends all about Mr Bull digging up the road.
George plays in the sandpit with Richard Rabbit and
Edmond Elephant.

On the way back, Peppa and George look forward to seeing Mr Bull again. But Mr Bull isn't there!
"He must have finished his work and gone home," says Mummy Pig.
George starts to cry.

"MOOOO! STOP!" It's Mr Bull!
"Is the water pipe broken again?" asks Peppa.
"No, this time it's a faulty electrical cable," says Mr Bull.
"How do you mend a frolty clackety crayble?" asks Peppa.
"WE DIG UP THE ROAD, OF COURSE!" says Mr Bull.
"Hooray!" cheer Peppa and George.

Everyone loves it when Mr Bull digs up the road!

START

Hole in the road.
Miss a turn.

Crane blocks the road.
Miss a turn.

Red light.
Miss a turn.

Chug-a-chug-a-chug-a

Toot! Toot!
Roll again.

Green light.
Go on two spaces.

Join in the race to get through all the roadworks. Take it in turns to throw a dice and move along the road, following the instructions on the way. The first person to reach the playground wins!

Mind the traffic cones! Go back one space.

FINISH!

Stop or Go?

Here's Mr Bull with his traffic light. Colour the top circle red if you want Mr Bull to STOP the traffic. Colour the bottom circle green if you want Mr Bull to let the traffic GO.

Dot-to-Dot Digger

George loves diggers. Join the dots, and colour in the scene to match the small picture.

Home at Last

Peppa and her family are almost home. Can you help them find the right road all the way up the hill to their front door?

a

b

c

Answer: Line C leads to the front door

Goodbye, Peppa

It's time to say goodbye! Goodbye, Peppa! Goodbye, George! See you again soon!

Before you go, do you know the answers to these questions about Peppa and her family?

Who is Peppa's teacher at playgroup?

What is George's favourite toy?

What colour is Peppa's dress?

Find the Fish!

Goldie Goldfish is Peppa and George's pet fish. Goldie usually lives in a bowl on top of Peppa's television, but she has been hiding on some of the pages of this book. Can you find her?

Colour in a fish each time you spot Goldie!

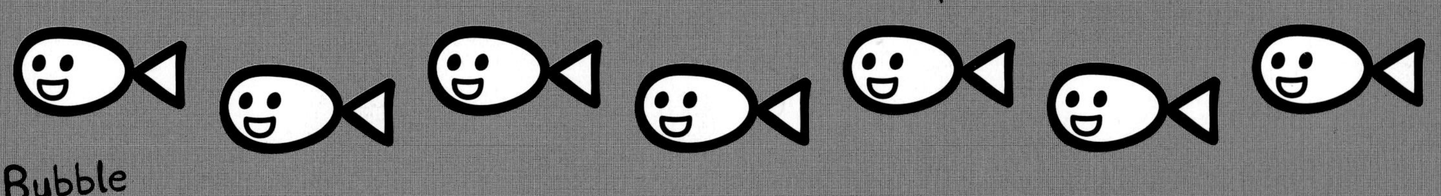

Bubble
Bubble

Answers: George's favourite toy is Mr Dinosaur, Peppa's teacher is Madame Gazelle and Peppa's dress is red

Look out for these other great Peppa Pig books!

Peppa Pig
Peppa's Dress-up
Sticker Book

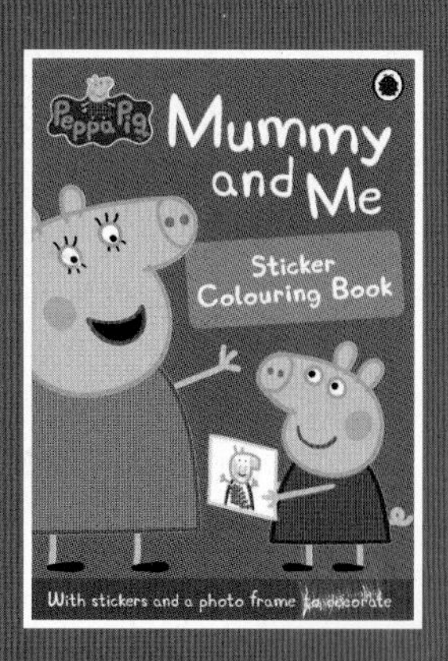

Peppa Pig
George's Racing Car

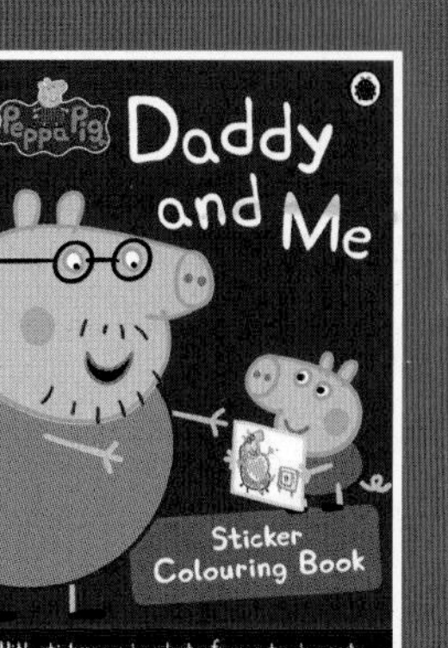

Peppa Pig
Colours
with Peppa

Practise with Peppa
Wipe-Clean
Counting
12
twelve bees